The Last Wish of the Mirror Queen

A Twisted Fairytale Sci-Fi Fantasy

RODA DUCOMMUN

COPYRIGHT

The Last Wish of the Mirror Queen
© 2025 Roda Ducommun
All rights reserved.

No part of this book may be reproduced, stored in a retrieval system, or transmitted in any form or by any means—electronic, mechanical, photocopying, recording, or otherwise—without the prior written permission of the publisher or author, except for brief quotations used in reviews or scholarly works.

This is a work of fiction. Names, characters, places, and incidents are products of the author's imagination or are used fictitiously. Any resemblance to actual events, locales, or persons, living or dead, is purely coincidental.

First edition: June 2025
Cover design by Roda Ducommun
Interior formatting by Roda Ducommun

For information or permissions, contact:
rodaducommun@gmail.com

Printed in the United Kingdom
ISBN: 978-1-7390892-2-1

DEDICATION

To Mark,
My constant in all worlds, mirrored or otherwise.

To Claude and Ava,

May you always find courage to face the unknown, discover the light in unexpected places, and bravely write your own story with the best versions of yourselves. And remember, even the smallest shard reflects the whole thing.

TABLE OF CONTENTS

CHAPTER ONE

The Last Echo

In the Kingdom of Everturn, time did not move forward. It spiraled—looping endlessly, like the carvings on the obsidian trees or the whispering winds in the Hollow Woods. Every night, stars flickered in strange patterns, as if trying to send a warning no one could decode. Every morning, the sun rose in a different hue: lavender, gold, once even black.

And somewhere near the edge of nowhere, a girl made of glass was born. Her mother hides a dangerous truth.

She was not born crying, but humming—a low, haunting note that shattered the air around her. Her skin was smooth as polished crystal, but within her veins, flickered circuitry instead of blood. Her eyes were twin moons of pale blue, glowing faintly in the dark.

The villagers feared her. They gave her no name at first, only whispers.

> **"Spawn of the Mirror Queen."**
> **"That which slipped through the crack."**
> **"Child of the Broken Spiral."**

"It's the Mirror Queen's curse," whispered the baker's wife, clutching her apron like a talisman. "She's returned."

But Elara didn't care for curses or kings or the hushed hatred that followed her down cobbled roads. She only wanted answers. Why did she dream of voices not her own? Why could she see glimpses of people who no longer existed? Why did she remember a mother who never gave birth to her—and a starship crumbling above a dying planet?

Time did not pass in Everturn. It folded.

Sunlight rose and fell in a loop, the spiral sun arcing across the sky like clockwork—but always in the same curve, No one aged. No crops rotted. No wounds lingered long enough to scar. Everything healed or forgot itself.

Everything but Elara.

She had appeared beneath the Spiral Tree sixteen spirals ago—a girl not born, but found. Her skin shimmered faintly like moonlit glass. Her eyes, too large for a child, held galaxies she had never seen. On her left wrist, embedded under translucent flesh, glinted a sliver of mirror that never dulled, never slept.

She named herself Elara, after a word she once dreamed—spoken by a woman with a crown of circuitry and tears that burned through time.

Elara sat beneath the Spiral Tree now, legs crossed, eyes closed, palm on the grass.

She could hear it: the hum. It ran beneath the soil, under the roots, beneath the village stone. A low vibration like a great machine sleeping just beneath the world. No one else seemed to feel it. But Elara lived by it. Breathed it.

And sometimes, the hum spoke back.

Today, it said:

"They're coming."

Elara opened her eyes.

High on the hill where time looped differently, two shadows had appeared—riders cloaked in fractured black glass. Their mounts did not gallop but glided, hooves never touching the ground. Behind them, a figure drifted above the grass, faceless and flickering like broken light.

Her breath caught. The shard in her wrist pulsed once.

Back in the village, the Spiral Bell tolled—three times. No one rang it. It hadn't sounded in years. People stepped out of their homes, confused. Afraid.

Elara rose, brushing grass from her dress. She turned, slowly, to face the riders.

They had come for her. She had always known they would.

The last child of a forgotten Queen. A spark left over from a collapsed destiny. An echo that should not have survived.

From the sky above, the spiral sun froze.
Time, in Everturn, skipped.

And Elara began to remember.

The Shard and the Spiral

Elara Mirth had never seen a real mirror. Not since the Collapse.

She had glimpsed one once, as a child—just a glint of silver buried in the sand like a dying star—but the scavengers took it before she could even touch the frame. In the Spiral, mirrors were contraband. Too many had gone mad staring into them, whispering to their reflections until their minds cracked like old glass.

Now, at sixteen, Elara stood knee-deep in rubble, staring at what could only be described as a forbidden miracle.

A mirror shard.

It pulsed with a faint, icy glow from beneath the fractured tiles of the old metro station. The underground structure was long abandoned, covered in ash and static dust, its columns corroded by time and quiet wars. Yet here, like a ghost waiting to be found, the shard called to her.

She crouched.

"Don't touch it," whispered Lark, the scavenger boy who'd guided her this far. His voice trembled, whether from fear or awe, she couldn't tell.

Elara ignored him. Her fingers hovered inches from the shard. The air around it shimmered like heat mirage, distorting her face into strange angles—older, younger, stranger.

"Why's it glowing?" she asked, not expecting an answer.

"No idea," Lark said. "But anything that still shines in the Spiral either wants to kill you or claim you. Probably both."

She reached anyway.

The moment her skin brushed the glass, pain shot through her palm—a burning jolt that zipped up her arm and behind her eyes. The world flickered. Not just in the way old lights do, but like a simulation buffering, stuck between frames.

She gasped.

The station vanished.

The world around her folded in on itself like paper. She fell—not through space, but through memory. Voices rushed past her ears: lullabies, warnings, screams. Somewhere, a clock was ticking backward.

And then—

Stillness.

Elara awoke in a field of white petals, beneath a silver sky stitched with black veins.

She sat up slowly. Her palm still stung, and when she looked, the mirror shard had embedded itself in her hand—like a puzzle piece melted into her flesh. The wound shimmered faintly, pulsing in sync with her heartbeat.

She wasn't in the Spiral anymore.

This place… it looked like a dream half-remembered. The trees were too tall, their bark etched with symbols she couldn't read. The air smelled like ink and ozone.

Then she saw it: a tower in the distance, crumbling but proud, with glass windows that caught no light.

Something inside her stirred. A whisper—not a voice, but a feeling.

Find the Mirror Queen.

Before she could process what that meant, a howl echoed through the forest.

Mechanical. Animal.

She turned, and from the tree line emerged a shadow cloaked in binary static, its eyes glowing with fractured light. A figure followed behind it, wrapped in tattered armour, face hidden by a mirrored visor.

The hunter and the machine. Watching her.

Waiting.

Elara did what she always did when the world turned upside down.

She ran.

🌀 *End of Chapter One*

CHAPTER TWO

The Binary Huntsman

Elara meets the enigmatic Binary Huntsman, a being made of both code and myth, who helps her activate the shard. He hints at the Spiral, the Queen, and a war of mirrors. Elara learns she may not be fully human.

They stood at the edge of Everturn, where the spiral fields dissolved into mist, and time ran thin.

Elara's feet crunched on silver grass, each step ringing faintly, like a chime only she could hear. Her wrist shard pulsed faster now—heat blooming beneath her skin. The hum that lived under the world had grown louder, more urgent. It wasn't warning her.

It was waking her.

Ahead, the three figures descended through the mist. The two riders peeled away, vanishing into mirrored streaks of light. But the one in the center remained, floating inches above the ground.

Elara's breath misted, though the air was not cold.

The figure landed soundlessly.

She saw no face. His helm was smooth black glass, shaped like an hourglass tipped sideways. Every part of him shimmered like oil on water—shifting, fluid, anchored to no time at all. On his back hung a blade made of broken seconds, ticking softly in reverse.

He took one step toward her.

"Elara," he said. His voice echoed in binary tones, as if layered with thousands of other versions of himself. "Anomaly confirmed."

She didn't speak. The shard in her wrist seared like fire. Her fingers trembled. The world around them slowed, dipped, folded.

The Huntsman raised his hand. "You are not meant to be."

"I didn't ask to be," Elara said, steadier than she expected.

"Deviation must be corrected."

Behind her, the Spiral Bell rang again.

And then the shard... shattered open.

Not outward—but inward. A beam of white fractured light tore through her chest, pulling memory and shadow and light together in a swirl of faces and fragments.

She saw a woman screaming in a war of mirrors.
She saw a boy with his eyes leaping into fire.
She saw a crown shatter on a tower of glass.
She saw herself.

And then—

She was elsewhere.

A forest. But not a forest.

The trees were data streams—branches of light coded in twisting helixes. Leaves like shards of memory. A breeze moved like static. The sky was a canvas of fractured clocks.

Elara stood inside the Mirror Engine.

"You activated it," said a voice behind her.

She turned.

The Huntsman was there—but not attacking. His faceplate was cracked now, and behind it, she saw—

A face. Human. Young. Sad.

"You're not just a hunter," she whispered.

He nodded once.

"I was the first," he said. "The first to try to rewrite the spiral. The Queen made me into this. To hunt myself. And now... you."

Elara clutched her wrist. The mirror shard was whole again—but different. It shimmered with a new layer of light. Her pulse synced with it, like music and memory.

"She's trying to overwrite me," she said, realization dawning. "Like she did you."

"Yes. But your thread is not yet bound. You can still diverge."

"Why are you telling me this?"

The Huntsman paused. A flicker of light passed through his cracked helm.

"Because once," he said, voice almost breaking, "I was you."

The forest split.

The Mirror Queen's laughter rang through every leaf, every data root.

"Little Elara," she whispered from everywhere and nowhere, "you cannot escape your own reflection."

The Huntsman turned toward the sound. His armor began to dissolve, pixel by pixel.

"Elara—run," he said. "Find the anchor. Find your story."

"But—"

He reached into his chest and tore free a key of light. "This unlocks the vault of beginnings. Where all stories loop. Take it."

The key burned in her hand.

"Go now."

The last thing she saw as she fell back into herself was the Huntsman drawing his reverse blade… and charging into the dark.

Elara awoke at the Spiral Tree, gasping.

In her hand was the key.

In her mind, the forest.

In her wrist, the mirror pulsed—no longer a shard, but a gateway.

The first gate had opened.

The Spiral was no longer safe.

And the Queen… knew she was awake.

⊚ End of Chapter Two

CHAPTER THREE

The Vault of Beginnings

They journey to the Vault, where rewritten fates are stored. Elara sees her own future written hundreds of ways—many ending with her becoming the Mirror Queen. She refuses to accept any of them.

Elara didn't sleep.

She wandered.

The village was silent, the Spiral Bell long stilled. But the world felt cracked. The light was wrong—too soft, too stretched. The spiral sun above trembled at its edges, glitching for a heartbeat every few minutes.

She clutched the key in her hand.

It hummed faintly, in time with the mirror shard beneath her skin.

It wanted to be used.

She followed the pull. Past the Spiral Tree. Past the edge of the known. Into the Glimmering Wastes, where light curved and whispers lived in the wind.

The sky turned upside down there.

Her shadow walked above her, on a reflection of the land she crossed. A mirror-world superimposed on her own.

At the center of the wastes, she found a door.

It was not built. It simply was.

A tall arc of light, set into a black wall that did not exist until you saw it. Smooth as silence. Etched with a single phrase: **"All stories begin again."**

The key in her hand pulsed.

Elara stepped forward.

As the key touched the door, reality bent.
The world shattered—not like glass, but like a song reaching a final note.

And the Vault of Beginnings opened.

She floated through the gate, not walking but remembered.

Inside, the Vault was infinite.

Corridors spiraled outward in impossible directions. Books hung in midair, opened and turning their own pages. Memories bled into reality—children crying, battles frozen in starlight, names whispered like prayers.

The floor beneath her shimmered with every step, reshaping itself to her thought.

Choose a story, the walls whispered.
Or become one.

Elara moved carefully, following an unseen thread.

The Vault responded.

A hallway opened.

A sphere of black crystal waited at the end, surrounded by floating shards—tiny reflections of her. In one shard, she was older, crowned in light. In another, she was broken, a villain hunted across timelines. In another, she was never found at all—still waiting beneath the Spiral Tree.

Her hands trembled.

The crystal whispered.

To know yourself, you must unwrite her.
Begin at the point of fracture.
The day the Queen split the Spiral.

She stepped forward.

The sphere dissolved.

And Elara fell—

Into the past.

Not her own, but the Queen's.

She stood in a throne room made of mirrored obsidian. Stars hung outside the windows, though no sky surrounded them. Machines hummed softly. At the center, the Mirror Queen knelt before a massive engine—the Mirror Core— alive with light and calculation.

"Too many timelines," the Queen said, voice raw. "Too much suffering. If I can erase the worst, collapse the deviations—"

"Then you erase people," said a voice behind her.

Elara turned.

It was the Huntsman. Human. Whole. Still just a man.

The Queen looked at him, tears like silver thread tracing her cheeks.

"I only wanted peace."

"Then let us live it," he said. "Without becoming gods."

"I cannot. I've already seen the end. If I don't control it, I become her."

"You already are."

The Queen touched the mirror in her hand—and shattered herself.

Elara screamed.

She landed hard, back in the Vault.

The shards spun around her, faster now.

Each showed a version of the Queen. Younger. Older. Mad. Merciful. Alone. Worshipped. Burned.

And then one shard—one only—glowed white.

A blank one.

Unwritten.

Elara reached for it.

The shard merged into her chest.

The others vanished.

The Vault pulsed once—and sealed shut behind her.

She now carried a blank thread. A timeline unanchored.

The beginning… was hers.

Back in Everturn, the spiral sun cracked down the middle.

The villagers fled indoors, praying to gods that no longer answered.

And in the mirror beyond time, the Queen opened her eyes.

She had felt it.

A thread she could not control.

"Elara…" she whispered, with something that might have been fear.

"You found the Vault."

"Now let's see if you can survive it."

🌀 End of Chapter Three

CHAPTER FOUR

Threads Unbound

Elara makes her first rewrite by altering a mirror-thread. Reality shifts. The Queen becomes aware. The Spiral begins to collapse. Elara loses the Binary Huntsman in the chaos, and time unspools.

Elara stood at the edge of the Vault's threshold.

The blank shard inside her pulsed like a newborn star.

Everything was too quiet now. No whispering walls. No reflections. No pathways. Only her, a key with no lock, and a memory that didn't belong to her.

The beginning is yours, the Vault had said.
But the Spiral never forgets its weavers.

She stepped forward—and the ground split.

Not broken. Unmade.

Reality twisted, refusing to hold. The path beneath her feet curled like paper touched by flame. Time flowed sideways. Stars reversed their burn. The world behind her collapsed into static.

She was in an unthreaded space.

A null realm.

Her feet found footing only because she willed it so.

"I exist," she whispered.

The words helped. Her thoughts anchored her shape. Her body reformed in pieces, solidifying from belief. Breath. Skin. Voice. Name.

Elara.

The null realm responded. Threads sparked in her wake—flickers of possibility.

One showed her as Queen.
Another as prisoner.
A third as fire, consuming the Spiral whole.

Too many paths.

Too many versions of herself.

And yet... none of them true.

She had to choose.

A **sound** tore through the void. Sharp and rhythmic.

Footsteps.

Elara turned—and saw them.

Weavers. Not people. Not exactly. They were remnants of broken timelines, scavengers of unwritten paths. Wraithlike. Faces blurred. Cloaked in strands of deleted futures. They smelled of burnt paper and forgotten names.

Their leader stepped forward—taller, faceless, wrapped in decaying threads.

"Elara of the Blank Thread," it rasped. "You carry the key to chaos."

"I carry a choice," she said, trying not to tremble.

"Then choose wrong. And end this Spiral."

They raised their hands. Threads shot toward her—barbed, sharp, hungry. Not to bind, but to overwrite.

Elara flung her hand forward—

The blank shard responded.

A wave of white erupted from her palm, burning the threads to ash. One Weaver disintegrated instantly. The others howled, retreating through folds in time.

She didn't know what she had done.

Only that it worked.

The shard in her chest had become a weapon.

Or maybe a wish.

She ran. Or maybe she dreamed of running.

The null realm shifted. Became places she had never seen but somehow remembered:

- A city in the sky, collapsing in reverse.
- A spiral library whose books screamed when opened.
- A version of Everturn where her mother wore the Queen's crown and wept black tears.

Each realm blinked in and out.

All collapsing.

Someone was deleting timelines.

Thread by thread.

And she knew exactly who.

The Queen sat on her mirrored throne in the **Heart of the Spiral**, watching it all.

Every path Elara touched.

Every alternate fate.

She held a string between two fingers—thin, golden, trembling.

Elara's new thread.

"It is unbound," said a voice beside her—one of her Echoes.

"And that makes her dangerous."

"No," the Queen said softly. "That makes her mine."

She snapped her fingers.

A portal opened.

From it stepped the Binary Huntsman—fractured now, glitching with every breath.

But his eyes were his own.

"She has touched the Vault," the Queen said. "And now she believes herself rewritten."

"She is."

"No," the Queen smiled. "She is remembering. I did not erase her. I scattered her."

The Huntsman said nothing.

"I want her returned," the Queen whispered. "Alive."

"Why?" he asked.

"Because only Elara can open the final gate."

Elsewhere, Elara collapsed at the edge of a dying timeline.

Breathing hard. Shaking.

The blank shard inside her dimmed.

She couldn't keep doing this. Couldn't keep running between threads without anchoring.

"I need help," she muttered.

And that's when the **Child of Ink** appeared.

A girl. No older than nine. Dressed in torn parchment and bound in writing that shimmered with moving letters.

She looked up at Elara with eyes that had read every story.

"You're lost," the child said simply.

"I'm unwritten," Elara replied.

"Then let's write something."

⊚ End of Chapter Four

CHAPTER FIVE

The Clockwork Market

Elara travels alone through a reality now unstable. She confronts memories of alternate selves and hears the Queen's voice calling from the depths of the Spiral. Her mother vanishes without a trace.

The Child of Ink led Elara through a doorway that wasn't there.

Not through space, but story.

The landscape shifted with each step—crumbling ruins flickering into palaces, deserts blooming briefly into forests before wilting into ice. Each scene flickered like sentences rewritten too fast.

"You're between drafts," the Child said, skipping over a bridge made of floating letters. "Nothing here is final until you choose."

Elara followed cautiously. Her legs ached from crossing collapsing realities. But here, in this in-between space, the ground felt… possible.

Like it was waiting for her.

The Child turned suddenly. "You carry the blank shard, right? The one not written yet?"

Elara nodded. "It bonded with me. In the Vault."

"Good," the Child said, her smile stretching just a little too wide. "Then you can make a rewrite."

"A what?"

"A single change. Any change. Big or small. One truth to bend the thread in your favor." She reached into her parchment tunic and pulled out a long, curling scroll. "Every thread has a cost. But the first rewrite is free."

Elara stepped forward slowly. The scroll shimmered, alive with flickering text. Names. Events. Worlds.

Near the bottom, a line blinked empty.

WRITE HERE.

"What should I change?" Elara asked, her voice tight.

The Child just shrugged. "What do you want most?"

That question held more weight than Elara expected.

She thought of her village—Everturn, now probably overrun with fear.

She thought of the Queen's throne room, the shards of possibility spinning like knives.

She thought of her mother.

"My mother," Elara said softly. "I want to know the truth. Who she really was. What she was hiding from me. Why she feared mirrors."

The scroll accepted her thought before she could write.

The ink moved.

Rewrite Confirmed:

In Timeline 7, Elara's mother confesses her origins before the Spiral cracks.

The scroll curled tightly and vanished in a puff of golden dust.

The Child of Ink clapped her hands. "Done!"

Elara staggered. The shard inside her pulsed hot—too hot.

"I don't feel different—" she began, but then the world rippled around her.

The ground buckled. The sky cracked.

Reality stitched itself anew.

And she was pulled back—not just through space or time, but narrative.

Into a new thread.

She gasped awake in the woods just outside Everturn.

The sky was still spiral-bound. The village still intact.

She was in **Timeline 7.**

A slight chill hung in the air, a warning of what was coming.

She ran.

Toward home.

Through familiar paths that felt slightly... off. A cottage door that opened the wrong way. A neighbor who waved with the opposite hand. Tiny things. But enough to remind her this was no longer the original thread.

This was a rewrite.

She burst into her house.

And there her mother stood—alive, pale, startled.

"Elara?" she whispered. "But... the Spiral said you were lost."

"I was," Elara said. "But I need to know. Who were you? What were you hiding?"

Her mother looked away. Then, with trembling fingers, reached into a box beneath the floorboards and pulled out a cracked mirror.

One Elara had never seen before.

"Look," she whispered.

Elara did.

And saw **the Queen's face** looking back at her.

Not present. Not future.

Past.

"You were her," Elara whispered. "Or… part of her."

Her mother nodded. "She broke herself. Scattered her essence across timelines. I was one of those shards. A remnant who escaped. I fled here. Raised you to be safe."

"I'm her too," Elara whispered, the blank shard inside her burning now like a truth finally spoken.

"Maybe," her mother said gently. "But maybe not. That's the gift of the blank thread. You're the first version that might escape her."

Before Elara could speak again, the windows shattered.

And through them came the **Binary Huntsman.**

This time not fractured. Not glitching.

Composed. Focused.

He looked at her mother. Then at Elara.

"You rewrote a truth," he said.

"I had to," Elara said.

"Then you've just marked this thread."

"What does that mean?"

The Huntsman held out a silver coin, etched with mirrored glyphs.

"This version of you... is now visible to her."

The Queen.

"She'll send more than Weavers now," he said grimly. "She'll come herself."

He dropped the coin in Elara's hand.

A ripple passed through it.

"Hold on to this," he said. "It's a key to the next gate."

Then he turned to smoke and vanished.

Elara stood, shaking.

Her mother stepped closer and placed a hand on her cheek.

"Whatever happens next," she said softly, "you're not her anymore."

And outside, the Spiral cracked louder.

⊚ End of Chapter Five

CHAPTER SIX

Queen of Glass and Code

The Mirror Queen arrives, walking through reflections of people long gone. She offers Elara a place beside her. Elara refuses and uses the shard to cause a greater Rewrite—splitting the Spiral further.

The Spiral bled light.

Above Everturn, the sky trembled—fractured into concentric rings, like ripples in a broken pond. Mirrors began appearing in the air, unanchored and floating, reflecting moments that had never happened and people who never were.

Time had turned inward.

Something—or someone—was forcing its way through.

Elara stood at the forest's edge, coin clenched in her fist, watching the threads tear like silk in fire. The **Binary Huntsman** was gone, and her mother had vanished with the sunrise, leaving behind only the cracked mirror and a letter Elara wasn't ready to read.

The silence was too heavy.

Then came the first bell.

A sound no one in Everturn had heard before.

A mirror-bell. Cold and hollow.

It meant the Queen was near.

The villagers didn't see her arrive.

They saw their mothers, their dead children, their younger selves, walking slowly through the square. Each one touched a mirror hanging impossibly mid-air—and vanished.

Reflected. Absorbed. Taken.

The Queen **walked without walking**. She stepped between timelines like turning pages in a story written in fire. Her robes were embroidered with memories she'd stolen. Her skin shimmered like a prism in collapse. Her eyes held *every version* of Everturn—burning, broken, blissful, barren.

She arrived not with a scream, but a sigh.

"She has rewritten," she said, voice folding through layers of time.
"And that cannot stand."

Elara felt her presence like a tide of dread.

She didn't wait.

She ran.

Into the Spiral Grove—the place where children dared not play, where no birds sang, where even trees grew in spirals too tight to climb. The blank shard in her chest pulsed brighter than ever, as if sensing its other half had finally arrived.

She turned a corner—and the Queen was there.

Waiting.

Not on a throne, but beneath a silver-barked tree shaped like a question mark.

She was not towering. Not monstrous. She looked… familiar.

Like an older version of Elara, refined by sorrow and sharpened by time.

Elara stopped in her tracks.

"You're not supposed to be here," she said.

"I was always here," the Queen replied. "You just finally remembered."

"What do you want?"

The Queen smiled softly. "You. Whole. Returned."

"I'm not a shard," Elara said, trembling. "I'm not a rewrite. I'm me."

"Then prove it," the Queen said.

She raised her hand.

The mirrors circling her flew toward Elara—each one holding a different Elara inside:

- One who never touched the shard and lived a quiet life.
- One who became Queen willingly and ruled the Spiral.
- One who destroyed the Vault.
- One who died as a child.
- One who stood beside the Queen, not against her.

Each version screamed across the glass, begging her to step in.

The Queen spoke gently.

"Pick one. And this ends. You'll return to a thread. You'll be anchored. Safe."

Elara looked at the mirrors.

And whispered, "No."

The Queen blinked. Just once.

"I don't want to choose someone else's ending," Elara said. "I want to write my own."

She threw the **coin** the Huntsman had given her.

It spun in the air—and struck one of the mirrors.

The glass didn't break.

It cracked reality.

The ground shook. The tree behind the Queen dissolved into letters. The other Elara-versions blinked out. The sky split—revealing pages of possibility beneath it.

The blank shard flared in her chest, syncing with the Queen's reflection.

For the first time, the Queen looked... startled.

"You don't understand what you've done," she hissed.

"I rewrote," Elara said. "And now I'll rewrite again. And again. Until I'm no longer you."

Lightning spiraled down from the skies—mirror-born and furious.

But Elara didn't flinch.

She reached into her chest and pulled the shard out.

It burned white-hot.

Not as a weapon.

As a **pen**.

"I write the next line," she whispered.

And touched the sky.

The world exploded in silence.

Not broken.

Unwritten.

◎ *End of Chapter Six*

CHAPTER SEVEN

The Fracture

Elara awakens in the Drafting Ground, where realities are shaped by sacrifice. She meets a younger self and faces the fact that every Rewrite comes at a cost. She prepares to make her hardest choice.

When Elara opened her eyes, the world was upside down.

Not metaphorically.

The sky hung beneath her feet, shimmering with mirrored lakes and reversed stars. Trees grew downward from clouds. Rivers flowed up into mountains, which hovered, suspended by nothing at all.

She had rewritten—but not restored.

She was somewhere between endings.

"Where am I?" she whispered.

The answer came in her own voice.

Not echoing. Not reflected.

But speaking **inside her head.**

"You opened the Rewrite Gate, Elara. Welcome to the Drafting Ground."

She clutched her chest—expecting the blank shard to still burn inside her—but it was gone. Or rather, not gone… *absorbed.*

"I didn't mean to come here," she said aloud.

"You did," her voice replied. *"You just didn't know what it meant."*

The trees whispered backwards as she walked. Her footsteps left no trail, but fragments of sentences—literal phrases—appeared behind her as she moved:

"…she chose differently this time…"
"…not all mirrors are prisons…"
"…some Queens are made, not broken…"

Elara's head spun.

"I need to find my way back," she said firmly.

"There is no back. Only forward. And forward depends on what you write next."

She walked across a glass bridge that hadn't been there a moment ago. It built itself from questions she hadn't asked yet. Beneath it flowed ink—not water—carrying scraps of stories written by people who'd lost their truths.

And there, in the middle of the bridge, sat a figure.

A girl. Maybe a shadow of one.

Thin, indistinct, as if only half-written.

Elara approached.

"Hello?" she called.

The girl turned.

Her face was Elara's.

But younger. **Innocent. Untouched.**

"Who are you?" Elara asked.

The girl didn't speak. She simply held out a torn piece of parchment.

Elara unfolded it.

It read:

"You cannot become whole until you choose what part to leave behind."

The girl blinked—and dissolved into falling words.

Elara stood alone again.

That night—if it could be called night—Elara found a place beneath a tree that wept ink instead of sap. She sat in its shade and tried to remember who she was. But the more she tried, the more versions of herself came rushing forward.

She saw herself in armor.
She saw herself on a throne.
She saw herself as the Queen.

"I am not her," Elara whispered.

"But you could be."

The voice again. Now softer. More seductive.

"You carry her blood. Her shard. Her defiance. You write like her."

"No," Elara said. "I write better."

The air vibrated. The Drafting Ground twisted.

And in front of her, a mirror rose.

Not floating. **Rooted.**

She saw herself.

But not the girl she was now.

She saw the Queen.

A single line appeared across the mirror's surface:

"What will you sacrifice to stay yourself?"

Then, her reflection stepped out of the glass.

The Queen version of Elara.

They stood face to face, no longer separated by time or fate.

"You've already changed more than you realize," the Queen-Elara said. "Every rewrite brings me closer."

"I'll undo you," Elara said.

"You'll become me."

"I won't."

The Queen smirked.

"Then prove it. Write the next choice."

The ground opened.

A quill rose.

No parchment. No ink.

Only a choice.

The Queen faded.

The Drafting Ground trembled.

And Elara understood:

The next rewrite wouldn't be free.

It would **cost her a memory.**

⊚ *End of Chapter Seven*

CHAPTER EIGHT

The Mirror Trials

To keep her sense of self and resist the Queen's pull, Elara must sacrifice a precious memory. She chooses to forget her father. As a result, she survives the Drafting Ground and rewrites herself—but becomes more alone.

Elara stood trembling, the quill in her hand pulsing with ghost-light. The words that would shape her next rewrite had not yet come to her lips.

The mirror behind her shimmered softly. Her other self—the Queen version—was gone. But not far. The Drafting Ground was quiet. Too quiet.

Then came the question again.

Not from a voice.

From **the air itself:**

"What will you sacrifice to stay yourself?"

A parchment unrolled mid-air in front of her—blank, but glowing. Waiting.

She knew now what this meant.

To forge a new rewrite—to make a real change—she had to give something up. Not a physical item. Not a promise. But a memory.

A piece of her life.

Of her *heart.*

Elara thought of all the memories she cherished:

- Her mother, tucking her in.
- Her first toy fox, worn and ragged.
- Laughing with the Binary Huntsman beside the fire.

And then she saw one.

A quiet afternoon in the attic, years ago.

She was five. Her father—who she barely remembered now—was brushing her hair and humming a song. He handed her a piece of broken mirror and said:

"No matter what happens, little light, you'll always see truth in the glass. Even when others lie."

Tears ran down her cheeks.

"No," she whispered. "Not that one."

But the quill glowed brighter.

The parchment shimmered.

"That is the cost," the Drafting Ground whispered. *"To forge a world where you don't become her—you must forget the one who taught you how."*

Elara's hand shook.

The quill dipped itself in nothingness—and wrote:

"She never met her father. And no one ever spoke of him."

The moment the ink dried, pain sliced through her mind.

The memory tore loose.

She screamed—but not out loud. It was a scream without sound. Her father's voice, his scent, his warmth, vanished like smoke in winter air.

The parchment folded.

The ground shifted.

And the Rewrite began.

When the world reassembled, she was standing back in the Spiral Grove.

No Queen.

No Binary Huntsman.

No ink-dripping trees.

Just the forest. Silent. Still.

A mirror hung before her. This one was **whole**.

And inside it, she saw **herself**—older, wiser, no longer fractured.

But she did not recognize the man standing behind her reflection.

He smiled at her. Kind eyes. Gentle hands.

"Who is that?" she whispered.

The mirror gave no answer.

Because Elara no longer remembered.

🌀 ***End of Chapter Eight***

CHAPTER NINE

Threads and Echoes

Back in Everturn, Elara notices the world has changed. Her choices echo through others. The Queen's power has weakened, but her presence lingers in the minds of those with mirror-sight.

The new Everturn looked the same—but it felt wrong. The air buzzed with silence. As if the wind remembered what the people had **forgotten.**

Elara wandered its pale stone streets, unseen. Or rather—forgotten.

Children skipped by her with mirror-paint smudged on their cheeks. Adults walked in looping routines. The sky overhead was clear, but the shadows cast **differently**—like glass, like memory.

She passed her home.

No one lived there now.

The red door still creaked on its hinges, but there were no signs of life. Not even a whisper of the laughter she once remembered. Her hand moved to knock, then stopped.

They wouldn't know her.

They **couldn't.**

She had written herself out of their lives.

Down in the town square, a traveling peddler displayed strange wares: charms shaped like fragments of broken glass, earrings that shimmered with kaleidoscope eyes. But it was the spinning mirror wheel behind him that caught her attention.

Each segment reflected a *different* possible version of Everturn:

- One where the sky was purple.
- One where children flew with wings.
- One where the Queen's symbol burned above every rooftop.

"Five wishes for a thread," the peddler said to a wide-eyed boy.

"Choose your echo. Choose your story."

Elara stepped closer.

The peddler's smile faltered as he caught her eye.

"You're not on the wheel," he said slowly.

"No," Elara replied. "I fell off it."

She noticed a symbol embroidered into his scarf. A sigil: twin moons over a cracked crown.

"You serve her," Elara whispered.

The peddler's hand trembled slightly.

"I serve the Spiral," he replied. "As do we all. Even the ones who try to escape it."

Elara turned, walking away before she lost her nerve.

She had expected the rewrite to erase the Queen's hold. Instead, it had only weakened the tether. The Spiral had evolved—**fractured further,** but not fallen.

And somewhere in the ripples of time and echo...

The Binary Huntsman lived again.

She felt it in her bones—more intuition than memory. A faint thread humming beneath her ribs. She followed it across fields, down forgotten roads, through dusk and dream.

She found him by a silver river, beneath a sky that wasn't quite real.

He stood barefoot in the water, humming a song she half-remembered.

His cloak was gone. His blades were gone.

But his eyes...

They were the same.

She stepped closer. "Do you remember me?"

He looked up.

A long silence.

"No," he said gently. "But… you feel familiar. Like déjà vu inside a dream."

Her throat tightened.

She could lie. She could tell him everything. But it would be *hers*—not his.

She sat beside him instead.

They watched the mirrorfish leap in pairs.

The sun dipped into the water and came up a moon.

"Do you ever feel like you were meant to do something… important?" he asked quietly.
"Like you were part of a story you can't quite remember?"

She nodded.

"All the time."

He turned to her. "Then maybe we find it together."

And Elara—who had given up her name, her past, her family—smiled for the first time in what felt like centuries.

Because sometimes, even in shattered stories, new threads begin.

⊚ End of Chapter Nine

CHAPTER TEN

The Spiral Rewritten

Elara finds the Huntsman again—rewritten, with no memory of her. She realizes she must give up her identity one last time to fully dissolve the Queen's tether to the world. She chooses a new name—and vanishes from history.

The Spiral shuddered.

Not with noise—but **absence.** Like silence had teeth.

Elara felt it as the Binary Huntsman slept beside the river, unaware that the strands of time were warping again—twisting to loop their fates into repetition.

She had one final mirror shard left.

It pulsed in her palm, not with light, but with weight—like a forgotten name pressing on her skin.

To break the Spiral,
she had to become the story's ending.

Elara returned to the Mirror Vale alone.

Each step was a choice.

With every echo she passed, the shard grew heavier, and so did her heart. The Vale shimmered in an eternal dusk, as if the world waited for her breath to drop the curtain.

And at its center...

The **Mirror Queen** stood.

She wore no crown now. Just shadows. Her reflection danced in every surface, an orchestra of regrets.

"You've returned," the Queen said. Her voice was softer. Sadder.

"I never left," Elara answered.

They circled each other like moons. Like memories.

"You rewrote the Spiral. Clever girl. But stories **fight** back. And so do I."

The Queen stepped closer, tilting her head.
"You look like me, you know. In the right light."

"I'm nothing like you."

"No? Then why are you still holding on to the shard? Why not destroy it?"

The Queen's eyes narrowed. "Because you want to remember. Even now."

Elara raised the shard. "You stole people's futures. You trapped them in roles they didn't choose."

"I gave them meaning," the Queen hissed. "I saved them from chaos. From irrelevance. Without story, what are we?"

"Free."

The Queen laughed, and the sound splintered mirrors across the Vale.

"You can't destroy me without becoming me," she said. "That's the final twist."

Elara looked into the shard. Not at the Queen.

But at **herself.**

Her real self.

The girl who once believed she wasn't special. Who ran errands for her family, tripped over her words, and read fairy tales by candlelight.

The girl who dared to ask for *one more wish.*

And she understood:
The Spiral wasn't just a prison. It was a promise.
A whisper that you could be more than you were.
Even if the cost was forgetting who you'd been.

She dropped the shard.

It didn't break.

It sank into the earth like a seed.

And from it bloomed a **mirror flower**—a fragile silver blossom, shimmering with echoes of every possibility that *hadn't yet been written.*

The Queen reached for it—

—but her fingers passed through like mist.

Elara stepped forward and whispered:

"I forgive you."

The Queen's form flickered.

"You can't."

"I just did."

With those words, the Vale fractured—not shattered, but unfolded.

Like a book reaching its final page.

Like a tale learning to let go.

The Queen vanished.

Not destroyed.

Released.

Elara woke by the river.

The Binary Huntsman stood beside her, holding a cup of sunwater.

"You disappeared," he said. "And then the sky blinked."

She took the cup. Drank.

"I ended the story."

He frowned. "You mean… finished it?"

"No," Elara said, smiling. "Set it free."

Later, they returned to Everturn together.

No one remembered the Mirror Queen.
No one remembered Elara.

But they remembered joy. Possibility.
They wrote new stories.

And in a garden by the old fountain, mirror flowers bloomed.

⊚ *End of Chapter Ten*

CHAPTER ELEVEN

The Forgotten Thread

In a distant town, a girl with no past writes stories into blank glass. Children gather to listen. The Queen is gone. Elara's tale is a rumor. But every time someone looks into a mirror and sees courage—they see her.

Somewhere beyond the Spiral...

A clock tower ticked backward.

Its hands moved with purpose, not time.

Inside the tower, a boy sat cross-legged on the floor. His eyes were stitched shut with silver thread, yet he saw more than most. He traced invisible lines across the wooden floor, humming a tune older than stars.

"Elara broke the story," a voice whispered through the gears.

"She ended the Queen," said another.

The boy shook his head slowly.

"No," he murmured. "She opened a door."

The tower began to vibrate. Dust rose from long-closed books. Mirrors cracked with hairline fractures—each one showing a different girl, a different Elara, in different worlds.

In one, she was a rebel in a city made of data.
In another, she wore the Queen's crown.
In one, she had never existed at all.

The Spiral doesn't die, the boy thought.
It adapts.

He reached into the floorboards and pulled out a book with no title.

Only a lock.

Only **his** name.

Cassian.

He was a Thread-binder.

One of the last.

And his task was just beginning.

Back in Everturn, Elara paused at the garden.

A single flower had wilted.
Its petals were darker than the rest—almost obsidian.

She bent to touch it and saw a flash:

A tower.
A blindfolded boy.
And a thread burning with her name.

"Elara," whispered the wind.
Or maybe it was memory.

She straightened, heart pounding.

Behind her, the Binary Huntsman laughed at something she hadn't heard.

But Elara stared into the horizon, toward something she couldn't name.

A story that hadn't been written.

Yet.

🌀 End of Chapter Eleven

Epilogue

In a realm between pages, where forgotten endings sleep…

The Mirror Queen watches.

Not in chains.

But with **wonder.**

For the first time, she does not know what happens next.

And that, she thinks, is a beautiful thing.

THE AUTHOR

Roda Ducommun is a new voice in twisted fantasy fiction. The Last Wish of the Mirror Queen is her debut short story — a haunting blend of fairytale and sci-fi that explores fractured identities, rebellion, and the secrets that lie behind every mirror. Roda writes from a place of deep imagination, always chasing the next world that waits just beyond reality. This is her first published work in the genre.

Thank you!

www.ingramcontent.com/pod-product-compliance
Lightning Source LLC
Chambersburg PA
CBHW072017170626
46813CB00005B/2173